Library of Congress Number: 75-19398

First printing, August 1974

Second printing, June 1975, Raintree Editions

Published by   **Raintree Editions**

A Division of Advanced Learning Concepts, Inc.
Milwaukee, Wisconsin 53203

Distributed by   Childrens Press
1224 West Van Buren Street
Chicago, Illinois 60607

Library of Congress Cataloging in Publication Data

CONTA, MARCIA MAHER.

Feelings between kids and parents.

SUMMARY: Explores the emotions involved in the
relationship between parent and child.

1. Emotions — Juvenile literature.   2. Parent and
child — Juvenile literature.   (1. Emotions.   2. Parent
and child)   I. Reardon, Maureen, joint author.
II. Rosenthal, Jules.   III. Title.
BF723.P25C66   1975   158'.24   75-19398
ISBN 0-8172-0045-2

Feelings
between Kids and Parents

Authors   Marcia Maher Conta
Maureen Reardon

Photography   Jules M. Rosenthal

I love to go to the library.

Today I saw a new book and I wanted
to read it right away.

But Mom said we didn't have time.

She said, "Let's check the book out and you
can read it when we get home."

I told Mom I couldn't wait that long.

Why is it parents don't want to do things
right away, like kids do?

5

"Get ready. Get set. Go!"

The race had just started and Mom
was already behind.

"Hey, you kids are too fast," she called.

"How can you pedal through this bumpy grass?"

My brother and I pedaled hard.

His bike is bigger and he won.

Why do parents sometimes let kids win?

When your mother is a dentist, you can't have
cookies and candy whenever you want.

Before we eat cookies we're supposed
to eat some fresh fruit.

But the cookies looked so good today
we decided to eat them right away.

Bob said, "Better hurry before Mom catches us."

Why are you unhappy when you do something wrong,
even if you don't get caught?

9

I asked Mom if I could watch a scary
TV program while she was gone.

"No, you'll have bad dreams," she said.

After she left, I asked Dad and he said,
"Sure, I'll watch the show with you."

You should have seen Mom's face when
she got home.

Boy! Was she mad.

Why do parents sometimes tell kids
two different things?

Dad and Mom decided to build a new house
in the country.

I told Dad, "I won't move. I'd miss
this house and my friends."

"Well," said Dad, "let's go out to see
the land we bought."

When we got there, he showed me what
I would see from my bedroom window.

Why is it parents don't seem
to mind moving?

This is my dad cooking at the firehouse.

All of the people there take turns
cooking and cleaning.

When I want to talk to Dad, I can go
to the firehouse.

But I can't sleep there.

It's against the rules.

Why do I need Dad the most when he's
staying overnight at the firehouse?

I live in the city with my mom.

My dad lives in a small town.

I stay with him on weekends.

Last week he took me to the circus.

He likes to make our time together special.

But sometimes I'd just like to
sit and talk to Dad.

Why can't I spend more time with
Mom and Dad together?

Yesterday when we went shopping, my brother Jerry wouldn't let me in the car.

That started a big fight. It was all his fault.

"Cut it out, Jerry!" I yelled. "Move over!"

"Both of you stop it or we'll stay
right here," said Mom.

Today Dad told us where we have to sit.

Why is it parents don't care
who started the fight?

I was really scared when I saw the snake.

Dad said, "Let's take a look at it, Pat. Pick it up in your hand."

I didn't want to touch it.

But Dad said, "It's just a garter snake. I had one for a pet when I was about your age."

Why are some things easier to do when Dad is around?

What do you think is in my sack? Gum? Candy?

No, just groceries.

I'm really mad.

I was good in the store. I didn't run around.

I thought Mom would buy me a treat for being good.

But she just said, "I was very proud of you
in the store, Billy."

Why don't I get a treat every time I'm good?

23

"Can I cut this part of the lawn, Dad?" I asked.

"Sure," said Dad. "Get your lawn mower out of the toy box."

"But I want to use the real mower," I said.

"Maybe next year."

"But you told me that last summer," I said.

Why is it parents always say, "You can, when you're bigger"?

My dad hadn't seen his friend Sam
for fifteen years.

They played on the same baseball team
in school.

Dad took me to meet Sam today.

"That's a nice looking kid you have, Ted,"
Sam said.

Then he said to me, "I'll bet you're a
batting champ like your dad."

I felt dumb. I didn't know what to say.

Why do parents like their kids
to meet their friends?

"How come you can go around the block
without asking your mom?" I asked Ben.
"I'm bigger than you and I have to ask."

Ben said, "But your mom lets you go
to the drugstore by yourself."

"But you get to stay up later," I said.

Why is it everybody's parents
seem to have different rules?

Can you believe my mom and dad get money
for riding bikes?

They work for the circus.

Sometimes when my parents are working
I get lonely.

I can't wait to get big enough to work
with them.

But Mom says, "What's important is
learning to work together as a family."

I guess that's the way it is with
other families too.

Design   **Interface Design Group, Inc.**

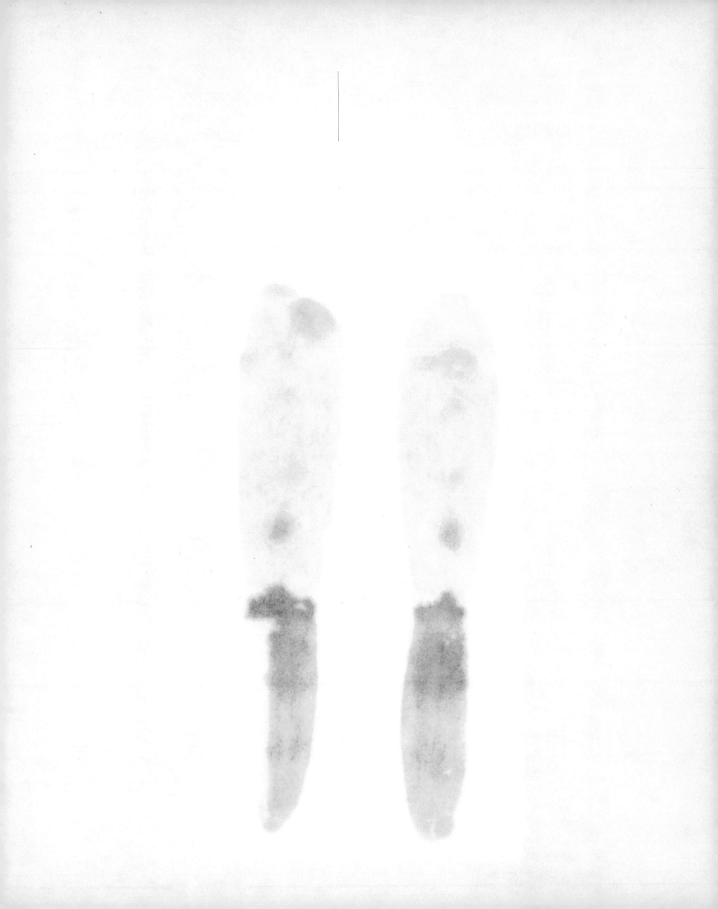

CURRICULUM MATERIALS
CENTER

JUV CPH SERIES RAINTREE
Conta, Marcia Maher
Feelings between kids and pare
nts

MAY 2 0 1985	MAR 1 7 1987		
OCT 0 2	MAY 5 '92 APR 5 1994		
FEB 1 8 1986	APR 2 5 1995		
APR 2 2 1986	DEC 12 00		
APR 2 9 1986			
MAY 1 3 1986			
MAR 1 0 1987			
MAR 1 7 1987			

Concordia College Library
Bronxville, NY   10708